THE GREAT PREHISTORIC SEARCH

Jane Bingham

Illustrated by Ian Jackson

Designed by Susie McCaffrey

Edited by Felicity Brooks

Scientific consultant: Professor Michael Benton

Contents

Hylonomus was the first known reptile to live on Earth. You can search for five of these early reptiles on pages 10 and 11.

About this book

This book is filled with exciting scenes from prehistoric times. You can use it to learn about dinosaurs and other creatures, but it's also a puzzle book. If you look carefully at the pictures, you'll be able to spot hundreds of prehistoric plants and animals. You can see below how the puzzles work.

This strip tells you when the animals in the picture lived.

Around the edge of the big picture are lots of little pictures.

The writing next to each little picture tells you the name of a creature. It also tells you how many creatures you can find in the big picture.

Although part of this dinosaur is outside the big picture, you should still count it.

You will have to look hard to spot these stegosaurs in the distance.

Sometimes, there are plants and trees to find.

This Ceratosaurus is shown from a different angle than the one in the little picture, but it still counts.

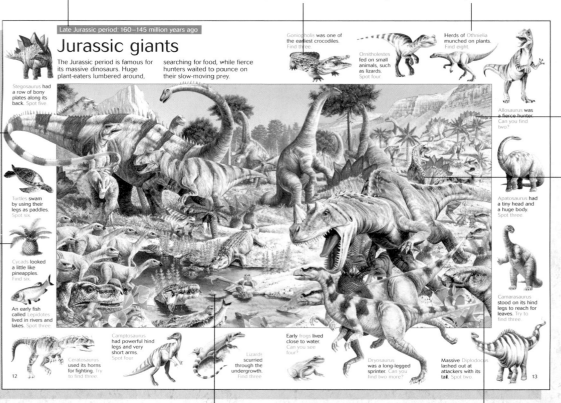

Late Jurassic period: 160–145 million years ago

Jurassic giants

The Jurassic period is famous for its massive dinosaurs. Huge plant-eaters lumbered around, searching for food, while fierce hunters waited to pounce on their slow-moving prey.

Stegosaurus had a row of bony plates along its back. Spot five.

Turtles swam by using their legs as paddles. Spot six.

Cycads looked a little like pineapples. Find six.

An early fish called Lepidotes lived in rivers and lakes. Spot three.

Ceratosaurus used its horns for fighting. Try to find three.

Camptosaurus had powerful hind legs and very short arms. Spot four.

Lizards scurried through the undergrowth. Find three.

Early frogs lived close to water. Can you see four?

Dryosaurus was a long-legged sprinter. Can you find two more?

Massive Diplodocus lashed out at attackers with its tail. Spot two.

Goniopholis was one of the earliest crocodiles. Find three.

Ornitholestes fed on small animals, such as lizards. Spot four.

Herds of Othnielia munched on plants. Find eight.

Allosaurus was a fierce hunter. Can you find two?

Apatosaurus had a tiny head and a huge body. Spot three.

Camarasaurus stood on its hind legs to reach for leaves. Try to find three.

12   13

Don't miss this frog, even though it's mainly underwater.

Although you can only see part of this dinosaur, it needs to be counted.

The challenge of these puzzles is to find all the animals and plants in the big picture. Some creatures look very similar so you will need to look carefully to spot the difference. If you get stuck, you can find the answers on pages 28 to 31.

To make the puzzles harder, each big picture shows lots of animals and plants very close together. But the prehistoric world wasn't really as crowded as this.

The prehistoric world

This book covers many millions of years. Its opening scene is set 545 million years ago, when life was just beginning in the oceans. Later came giant insects, fish and amphibians (creatures that could live on land and in water).

Trilobites were some of the first creatures to live in the oceans.

The first dragonflies were as large as seagulls are today.

This early fish swam in prehistoric swamps.

Frog-like amphibians existed 150 million years ago.

The first creatures to spend all their lives on land were reptiles. They had dry, scaly skin and laid eggs. The largest of all the reptiles were the dinosaurs.

Most dinosaurs were enormous. This foot belongs to a dinosaur that was twice the size of elephants today.

Rhamphorhynchus was a flying reptile that scooped up fish in its beak.

About 65 million years ago, all the dinosaurs died out and a new group of animals spread out across the Earth. These were mammals – animals with fur that fed their babies with milk. Gradually, different types of mammals developed around the world.

The first mammals scampered around under the feet of the dinosaurs. They looked like present-day shrews.

How do we know?

How do we know about the prehistoric world? For many years, experts, known as palaeontologists, have been finding and studying fossils. Fossils are the remains of prehistoric creatures and plants.

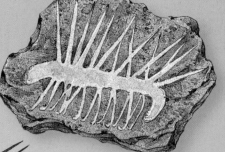

This fossil shows the outline of the sea creature Hallucigenia.

By studying fossils carefully, palaeontologists can work out how prehistoric creatures used to look and build up a picture of life on Earth millions of years ago.

The fossilized skull of Triceratops provides many clues about how the dinosaur looked and even what food it ate.

Strange names

When palaeontologists discover a new prehistoric creature, they give it a name. They choose Latin or Greek names that can be used in any country. Often, a creature's name is a good description of the way it looks or behaves.

This dinosaur is called Camptosaurus, which means 'flexible reptile' in Latin. It was given its name because of its supple neck and spine.

Prehistoric time

The Earth has existed for billions of years –
a length of time so vast it's impossible to
imagine. To make it easier to study the
Earth's history, experts have divided
prehistoric time into different periods.
Each period lasted for many
millions of years.

This diagram shows the
main periods of prehistoric
time. You can also see
when different animals
and plants first
appeared on Earth.

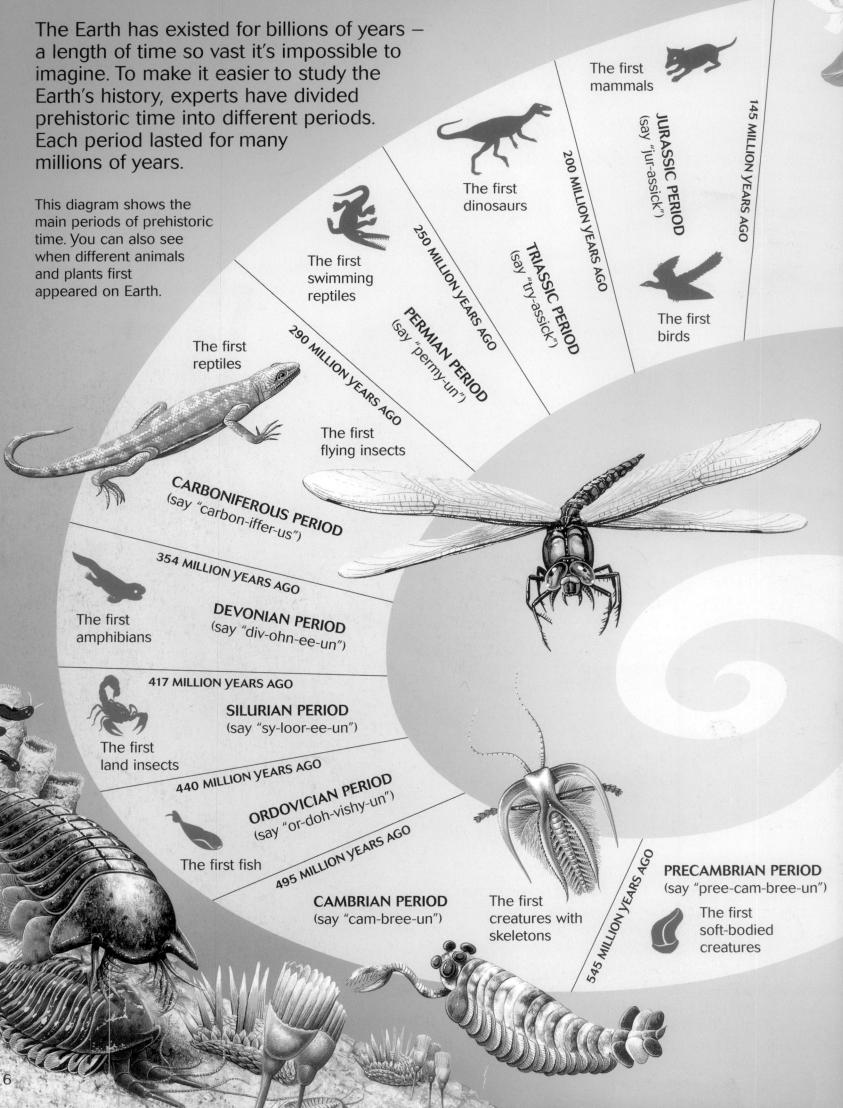

The first
mammals

JURASSIC PERIOD
(say "Jur-assick")

145 MILLION YEARS AGO

The first
dinosaurs

200 MILLION YEARS AGO

The first birds

The first
swimming
reptiles

250 MILLION YEARS AGO

TRIASSIC PERIOD
(say "try-assick")

PERMIAN PERIOD
(say "permy-un")

The first
reptiles

290 MILLION YEARS AGO

The first
flying insects

CARBONIFEROUS PERIOD
(say "carbon-iffer-us")

354 MILLION YEARS AGO

DEVONIAN PERIOD
(say "div-ohn-ee-un")

The first
amphibians

417 MILLION YEARS AGO

SILURIAN PERIOD
(say "sy-loor-ee-un")

The first
land insects

440 MILLION YEARS AGO

ORDOVICIAN PERIOD
(say "or-doh-vishy-un")

The first fish

495 MILLION YEARS AGO

CAMBRIAN PERIOD
(say "cam-bree-un")

The first
creatures with
skeletons

545 MILLION YEARS AGO

PRECAMBRIAN PERIOD
(say "pree-cam-bree-un")

The first
soft-bodied
creatures

Hallucigenia had two rows of spines on its back. Spot four.

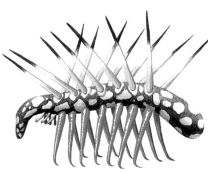

Dinomischus looked like a plant, but it was really an animal. Find 14.

Opabinia had five eyes on stalks and a long nozzle with claws at its tip. Spot three.

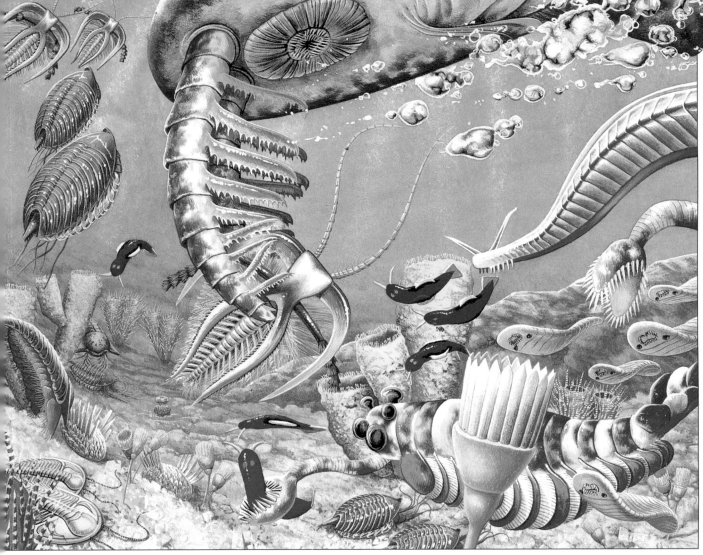

Anomalocaris grabbed small creatures in its claws. Can you see one more?

Amwiskia had a flattened body and two small feelers. Spot 10.

Aysheaia had spiky feet for clambering over sponges. Find nine.

Ottoia was a large worm that burrowed into the sea bed. Try to spot four.

Trilobites scuttled around, searching for food. Find three of each kind.

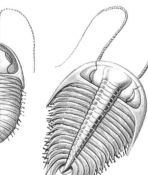

The shimmering scales of Wiwaxia warned off hunters. Spot six.

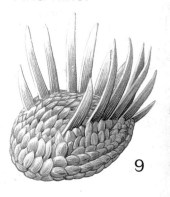

Forests and swamps

During the Carboniferous period, most of the Earth was covered in steamy forests. Giant insects crawled or flew through the forests, and strange water creatures lurked in swamps.

Giant scorpions used their deadly tails to sting their prey. Find four.

Platysomus swam by flicking its body from side to side. Spot 10.

Meganeura was as big as a seagull. Try to find three.

Snake-like Ophiderpeton spent most of its time swimming. Find three.

Arthropleura was a giant millipede that feasted on rotting plants. Spot three.

Cockroaches flew through the air or scuttled over the ground. Find 11.

Eryops looked like a small crocodile. Can you see five?

Early spiders wove simple webs to trap insects. Find four spiders.

Centipedes grasped their prey in their fangs. Spot five.

Keraterpeton used its long tail for swimming. Find six.

Tiny leaves sprouted from the stems of giant horsetails. Spot five.

Sigillaria had no branches, just a clump of leaves. Try to find six.

Towering Lepidodendron had a scaly trunk. Spot six.

Hylonomus is the earliest known reptile. It spent its life on land. Spot five.

Diploceraspis had a head shaped like a boomerang. Try to find four.

Tree ferns were plants that looked like palm trees. Spot three.

11

Jurassic giants

The Jurassic period is famous for its massive dinosaurs. Huge plant-eaters lumbered around, searching for food, while fierce hunters waited to pounce on their slow-moving prey.

Stegosaurus had a row of bony plates along its back. Spot five.

Turtles swam by using their legs as paddles. Spot six.

Cycads looked a little like pineapples. Find six.

An early fish called Lepidotes lived in rivers and lakes. Spot three.

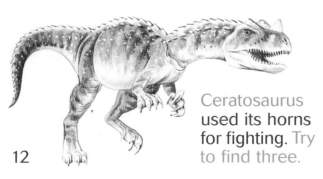

Ceratosaurus used its horns for fighting. Try to find three.

Camptosaurus had powerful hind legs and very short arms. Spot four.

Lizards scurried through the undergrowth. Find three.

12

Goniopholis was one of
the earliest crocodiles.
Find three.

Ornitholestes
fed on small
animals, such
as lizards.
Spot four.

Herds of Othnielia
munched on plants.
Find eight.

Allosaurus was
a fierce hunter.
Can you find
two?

Apatosaurus had
a tiny head and
a huge body.
Spot three.

Camarasaurus
stood on its hind
legs to reach for
leaves. Try to
find three.

Early frogs lived
close to water.
Can you see
four?

Dryosaurus
was a long-legged
sprinter. Can you
find two more?

Massive Diplodocus
lashed out at
attackers with its
tail. Spot two.

13

Oceans and skies

At the same time as the dinosaurs were living on land, enormous reptiles were swimming through the oceans and swooping through the skies. How many flying and swimming reptiles can you find?

Ichthyosaurus looked like a small dolphin. Try to spot five.

Early shrimps drifted through the water. Find six.

Peloneustes snapped up food in its huge jaws. Spot two.

Fast-flying Anurognathus chased after insects. Find six.

Cryptoclidus had long, flexible flippers. Can you see two?

Ammonites were protected by a spiral shell. Spot eight more.

Aspidorhynchus was an early hunting fish. Spot three.

Pterodactylus had wings like a bat. Spot three more.

Metriorhynchus was an early crocodile with a tail and flippers. Find three.

Belemnites had long, wavy suckers. Can you see 11?

Muraenosaurus waved its neck around, searching for food. Spot two.

Ophthalmosaurus had huge eyes to help it see underwater. Find three more.

Pholidophorus looked like a herring. Find 18.

Rhamphorhynchus scooped up fish in its beak. Find three.

Scaphognathus used its long tail to help it fly. Spot three.

Giant Liopleurodon was a very fast swimmer. Try finding two.

Cretaceous creatures

This scene shows some of the creatures that lived in Southern England during the early Cretaceous period. At the end of this period, about 65 million years ago, all the dinosaurs died out.

Dragonflies darted through the air. Try to find six.

Pelorosaurus lumbered over the plains. Spot seven.

Hylaeosaurus was covered with knobs and spikes. Find three.

Early seabirds flew overhead. Spot six.

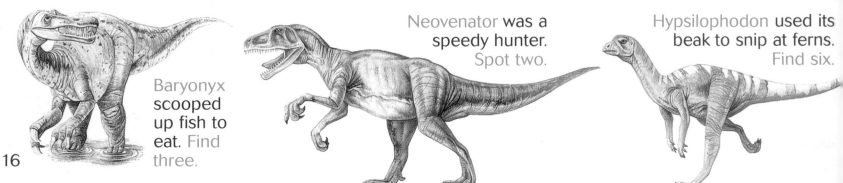

Baryonyx scooped up fish to eat. Find three.

Neovenator was a speedy hunter. Spot two.

Hypsilophodon used its beak to snip at ferns. Find six.

16

Ornithocheirus was a flying reptile with huge, leathery wings. Find four more.

Beetles crawled over leaves. Can you see 14?

Bernissartia was a tiny crocodile. Find five.

Early mammals scurried over the ground. Spot three of each kind.

Pond tortoises lived close to the water. Find six.

Vectisaurus had a ridge along its back. Can you see three?

Polacanthus was protected by bony plates and spines. Spot four.

Iguanodon had a large spike on its thumb. Spot six more.

After the dinosaurs

After the dinosaurs died out, many new mammals developed. Some were large and lumbering, but others were small and speedy. Climbing mammals lived in trees and early bats flew through the air.

Uintatherium was a massive creature with a very knobbly head. Find two.

Coryphodon loved to splash around in water. Spot four.

Patriofelis looked like a small panther. Can you see three?

Giant Diatryma was too heavy to fly. Try to find two.

Pristichampsus was a crocodile that lived on land. Spot two.

Stylinodon dug up roots to eat. Find five.

Icaronycteris was
an early bat. Spot
12 more.

Champsosaurus
caught fish in
its long jaws.
Find three.

Smilodectes could
leap from branch to
branch. Spot seven
more.

Diacodexis was
a fast runner.
Can you see
nine?

Ischyromys
climbed trees
like a squirrel.
Spot three.

Lively Chriacus
scampered
around, eating
insects and fruit.
Find four.

Hyrachyus was an ancestor
of the rhino. Spot four.

Tiny Hyracotherium
was the first horse.
Find six more.

Lizards and snakes
slithered through the
forest. Spot four of each.

19

In South America

Around 150 million years ago, South America became an island. It stayed cut off from the rest of the world for the next 145 million years. Some of its animals were unlike creatures anywhere else.

Peltephilus was covered with bony plates. Try to find two.

Rabbit-like Protypotherium bounded over the grassy plains. Spot five.

Large water snakes waited for their prey. Can you spot three?

Eocardia was a good swimmer. It lived near rivers and ponds. Find four.

Homalodotherium liked eating leaves. Sometimes it prowled around on all fours. Find two more.

Hapalops often hung upside-down from branches. Try to find three.

Homunculus could wrap its tail around branches. Can you spot six?

Butterflies flitted through the grasslands. Try finding 17 more.

Necrolestes used its nose to help it find insects to eat. Find two.

Astrapotherium lived on water plants. Can you see three?

Graceful **Thoatherium** looked like a small gazelle. Try to find nine.

Cladosictis hunted fish, reptiles and mice. Can you spot six?

Diadiaphorus looked like a very small horse. Try to find nine.

Theosodon had legs like a camel and a long nose. Can you spot four?

Phorusrhacos could run fast but couldn't fly. Find two.

Borhyaena had a pouch like a kangaroo. Spot two.

21

African animals

During the Miocene epoch, some very large animals lived in Africa. Early elephants roamed over the grassland, and hippos and rhinos wallowed in rivers. Can you find over 70 African creatures?

Giant hippos splashed around in rivers. Spot six.

Vultures flew overhead, searching for food. Find five more.

Dendropithecus swung through the trees. Can you see five?

Sivapithecus could stand on its hind legs. Spot six.

Platybelodon used its wide trunk to pull up water weeds. Try to find three.

Kanuites lived in trees as well as on the ground. Spot five.

Packs of hunting dogs chased after their prey. Find seven.

Teleoceras was an early rhino. Find two.

Aardvarks rooted around for insects to eat. Spot three.

Deinotherium was a giant elephant with downward-curving tusks. Find two.

Prolibytherium had large horns but was actually an early giraffe. Spot six.

Early ostriches could run very fast. Find four.

Tree snakes hung from branches. Spot four.

Hipparion was an early horse. Spot seven.

Afrosmilus was a cunning hunter that could climb trees. Can you see two?

Percrocuta fed on dead animals. Find four more.

A sticky end

Around 20,000 years ago, many creatures in California drowned in pits of tar. Others came to feed on them, but they became stuck as well. Here are some of the animals that drowned in the pits.

Herds of bison wandered over the grasslands. Can you see 10?

Camelops looked like a modern llama. Spot four.

Teratorns fed on dead and dying animals. Find six.

Western horses were smaller than horses today. Spot eight.

Giant sloths had bony lumps under their skin. Find two.

Weasels raced through the long grass. Spot five.

Eagles swooped down on their prey. Can you see four?

24

Frogs and toads were trapped in the tar. Find three of each.

Frog  Toad

Rattlesnakes could make their tails vibrate. Try to spot three.

Smilodon had huge, curved fangs. Spot two more.

Dire wolves hunted in packs. Can you see six?

Male turkey

Male turkeys had splendid tail feathers. Find three females and two males.

Female turkey

Storks flew in to join the feast. Find four.

Mammoths used their tusks to shovel up food. Spot six.

Icy wastes

During the Earth's long history, there have been several ice ages. At these times, large parts of the globe were covered by ice and snow. This scene is set in Russia during the last ice age.

Megaloceros was the largest deer that has ever lived. Spot three.

Great auks were birds that could swim. Can you see 12?

Arctic foxes were cunning hunters. Find three more.

Lemmings dug tunnels in the snow. Spot seven.

Bears often sheltered inside caves. Find three.

Sea cows had a layer of blubber to keep them warm. Find two.

Woolly rhinos were covered with thick hair. Spot two.

26

Enormous whales plunged
through the icy water.
Spot two.

Woolly mammoths
had a store of fat on
their heads. Find
five more.

Seals gave birth
to fluffy white
pups. Find five
adults and four
pups.

Arctic hares
were hard to
spot against the
snow. Spot five.

Shaggy musk
oxen roamed
over the snow.
Try to find six.

Arctic stoats could
squeeze through tunnels
after their prey. Spot four.

Reindeer fought
off hunters with
their horns.
Find 11 more.

Elasmotherium
had a huge horn
made from hair.
Find one more.

Prehistoric puzzles

Why not test your prehistoric knowledge by trying out these puzzles? You will probably need to look back through the book to find out the answers. If you are really stuck, you can look on page 32.

1. All of these dinosaurs except one hunted animals. Spot the plant-eater.

A   B   C   D   E

2. One of these creatures is not a bird. Do you know which one it is?

A   B   C   D   E

3. Can you guess which of these creatures is not a dinosaur?

A   B   C   D   E

Answers

The keys on the next few pages show you exactly where all the animals and plants appear in the scenes in this book. You can use these keys if you have a problem trying to find a particular creature or plant.

Crowded seas 8-9

Marrella, 1, 2, 3, 4, 5, 6

Pikaia, 7, 8, 9, 10, 11, 12, 13, 14

Sponges, 15, 16, 17, 18, 19

Jellyfish, 20, 21, 22, 23, 24, 25, 26, 27, 28

Leanchoilia, 29, 30, 31, 32, 33, 34

Odontogriphus, 35, 36, 37, 38, 39

Sanctacaris, 40, 41, 42, 43

Ottoia, 44, 45, 46, 47

Trilobites, 48, 49, 50, 51, 52, 53

Wiwaxia, 54, 55, 56, 57, 58, 59

Aysheaia, 60, 61, 62, 63, 64, 65, 66, 67, 68

Amwiskia, 69, 70, 71, 72, 73, 74, 75, 76, 77, 78

Anomalocaris, 79

Opabinia, 80, 81, 82

Dinomischus, 83, 84, 85, 86, 87, 88, 89, 90, 91, 92, 93, 94, 95, 96

Hallucigenia, 97, 98, 99, 100

Forests and swamps 10-11

Giant scorpions, 1, 2, 3, 4

Platysomus, 5, 6, 7, 8, 9, 10, 11, 12, 13, 14

Meganeura, 15, 16, 17

Ophiderpeton, 18, 19, 20

Arthropleura, 21, 22, 23

Cockroaches, 24, 25, 26, 27, 28, 29, 30, 31, 32, 33, 34

Eryops, 35, 36, 37, 38, 39

Hylonomus, 40, 41, 42, 43, 44

Diploceraspis, 45, 46, 47, 48

Tree ferns, 49, 50, 51

Lepidodendron, 52, 53, 54, 55, 56, 57

Sigillaria, 58, 59, 60, 61, 62, 63

Giant horsetails, 64, 65, 66, 67, 68

Keraterpeton, 69, 70, 71, 72, 73, 74

Centipedes, 75, 76, 77, 78, 79

Spiders, 80, 81, 82, 83

Jurassic giants 12-13

Stegosaurus, 1, 2, 3, 4, 5

Turtles, 6, 7, 8, 9, 10, 11

Cycads, 12, 13, 14, 15, 16, 17

Lepidotes, 18, 19, 20

Ceratosaurus, 21, 22, 23

Camptosaurus, 24, 25, 26, 27

Lizards, 28, 29, 30

Frogs, 31, 32, 33, 34

Dryosaurus, 35, 36

Diplodocus, 37, 38

Camarasaurus, 39, 40, 41

Apatosaurus, 42, 43, 44

Allosaurus, 45, 46

Othnielia, 47, 48, 49, 50, 51, 52, 53, 54

Ornitholestes, 55, 56, 57, 58

Goniopholis, 59, 60, 61

Oceans and skies 14-15

Ichthyosaurus, 1, 2, 3, 4, 5

Shrimps, 6, 7, 8, 9, 10, 11

Peloneustes, 12, 13

Anurognathus, 14, 15, 16, 17, 18, 19

Ammonites, 20, 21, 22, 23, 24, 25, 26, 27

Cryptoclidus, 28, 29

Aspidorhynchus, 30, 31, 32

Rhamphorhynchus, 33, 34, 35

Scaphognathus, 36, 37, 38

Liopleurodon, 39, 40

Pholidophorus, 41, 42, 43, 44, 45, 46, 47, 48, 49, 50, 51, 52, 53, 54, 55, 56, 57, 58

Ophthalmosaurus, 59, 60, 61

Muraenosaurus, 62, 63

Belemnites, 64, 65, 66, 67, 68, 69, 70, 71, 72, 73, 74

Metriorhynchus, 75, 76, 77

Pterodactylus, 78, 79, 80

Cretaceous creatures 16-17

Dragonflies, 1, 2, 3, 4, 5, 6

Pelorosaurus, 7, 8, 9, 10, 11, 12, 13

Hylaeosaurus, 14, 15, 16

Seabirds, 17, 18, 19, 20, 21, 22

Baryonyx, 23, 24, 25

Neovenator, 26, 27

Hypsilophodon, 28, 29, 30, 31, 32, 33

Vectisaurus, 34, 35, 36

Polacanthus, 37, 38, 39, 40

Iguanodon, 41, 42, 43, 44, 45, 46

Pond tortoises, 47, 48, 49, 50, 51, 52

Mammals, 53, 54, 55, 56, 57, 58

Bernissartia, 59, 60, 61, 62, 63

Beetles, 64, 65, 66, 67, 68, 69, 70, 71, 72, 73, 74, 75, 76, 77

Ornithocheirus, 78, 79, 80, 81

After the dinosaurs 18-19

Uintatherium, 1, 2

Coryphodon, 3, 4, 5, 6

Patriofelis, 7, 8, 9

Diatryma, 10, 11

Pristichampsus, 12, 13

Stylinodon, 14, 15, 16, 17, 18

Hyrachyus, 19, 20, 21, 22

Hyracotherium, 23, 24, 25, 26, 27, 28

Lizards and snakes, 29, 30, 31, 32, 33, 34, 35, 36

Chriacus, 37, 38, 39, 40

Ischyromys, 41, 42, 43

Diacodexis, 44, 45, 46, 47, 48, 49, 50, 51, 52

Smilodectes, 53, 54, 55, 56, 57, 58, 59

Champsosaurus, 60, 61, 62

Icaronycteris, 63, 64, 65, 66, 67, 68, 69, 70, 71, 72, 73, 74

In South America 20-21

Peltephilus, 1, 2

Protypotherium, 3, 4, 5, 6, 7

Water snakes, 8, 9, 10

Eocardia, 11, 12, 13, 14

Homalodotherium, 15, 16

Hapalops, 17, 18, 19

Theosodon, 20, 21, 22, 23

Phorusrhacos, 24, 25

Borhyaena, 26, 27

Diadiaphorus, 28, 29, 30, 31, 32, 33, 34, 35, 36

Cladosictis, 37, 38, 39, 40, 41, 42

Thoatherium, 43, 44, 45, 46, 47, 48, 49, 50, 51

Astrapotherium, 52, 53, 54

Necrolestes, 55, 56

Butterflies, 57, 58, 59, 60, 61, 62, 63, 64, 65, 66, 67, 68, 69, 70, 71, 72, 73

Homunculus, 74, 75, 76, 77, 78, 79

African animals
22-23

Hippos, 1, 2, 3, 4, 5, 6

Vultures, 7, 8, 9, 10, 11

Dendropithecus, 12, 13, 14, 15, 16

Sivapithecus, 17, 18, 19, 20, 21, 22

Platybelodon, 23, 24, 25

Kanuites, 26, 27, 28, 29, 30

Hunting dogs, 31, 32, 33, 34, 35, 36, 37

Hipparion, 38, 39, 40, 41, 42, 43, 44

Afrosmilus, 45, 46

Percrocuta, 47, 48, 49, 50

Tree snakes, 51, 52, 53, 54

Early ostriches, 55, 56, 57, 58

Prolibytherium, 59, 60, 61, 62, 63, 64

Deinotherium, 65, 66

Aardvarks, 67, 68, 69

Teleoceras, 70, 71

A sticky end 24-25

Bison, 1, 2, 3, 4, 5, 6, 7, 8, 9, 10

Camelops, 11, 12, 13, 14

Teratorns, 15, 16, 17, 18, 19, 20

Western horses, 21, 22, 23, 24, 25, 26, 27, 28

Giant sloths, 29, 30

Weasels, 31, 32, 33, 34, 35

Eagles, 36, 37, 38, 39

Turkeys, 40, 41, 42, 43, 44

Storks, 45, 46, 47, 48

Mammoths, 49, 50, 51, 52, 53, 54

Dire wolves, 55, 56, 57, 58, 59, 60

Smilodon, 61, 62

Rattlesnakes, 63, 64, 65

Frogs and toads, 66, 67, 68, 69, 70, 71

Icy wastes 26-27

Megaloceros, 1, 2, 3

Great auks, 4, 5, 6, 7, 8, 9, 10, 11, 12, 13, 14, 15

Arctic foxes, 16, 17, 18

Lemmings, 19, 20, 21, 22, 23, 24, 25

Bears, 26, 27, 28

Sea cows, 29, 30

Woolly rhinos, 31, 32

Reindeer, 33, 34, 35, 36, 37, 38, 39, 40, 41, 42, 43

Arctic stoats, 44, 45, 46, 47

Elasmotherium, 48

Musk oxen, 49, 50, 51, 52, 53, 54

Arctic hares, 55, 56, 57, 58, 59

Seals, 60, 61, 62, 63, 64, 65, 66, 67, 68

Woolly mammoths, 69, 70, 71, 72, 73

Whales, 74, 75

Index

Additional illustration: Inklink Firenze
Picture credit: p7, ©Digital Vision

Answers to prehistoric puzzles: 1. **D** Camarasaurus, 2. **B** Anurognathus, 3. **D** Peloneustes